AND THEN IT
HAPPENED

.. 8 ..

M & L Wade

Books For Boys Inc.

©2008

ISBN: 978-0973117875

Printed in Canada by Hignell Book Printing

Books For Boys Inc.
P.O. Box 87
Strathroy ON N7G 3J1

Contents

Chapter 1 The Dirty Rotten Grandma!............................. 1

Chapter 2 The Substitute...7

Chapter 3 Three On Three...13

Chapter 4 The Snake..23

Chapter 5 The Three 'Bares'...34

Chapter 6 Outhouse With A View.......................................42

Chapter 7 Gordon to the Rescue...45

Chapter 8 The Talent Show Disaster..................................51

Chapter 9 Gordon's Lesson..59

Chapter 10 Easy Come, Easy Go.......................................73

Chapter 11 Hamburger Helper...81

Chapter 1

The Dirty Rotten Grandma!

Next to Christmas, birthdays are one of the best days of the year; not because it was the day you were born, but because you get presents! Two days ago it was Gordon's birthday, and his Uncle Ivan gave him $100.00 to take Paulo and me to a football game in the city. My dad agreed to drive us, and early Saturday morning we piled into the back of the car, full of excitement.

"The tickets are $30.00 each," said Gordon, "which leaves us $10.00 left over for drinks."

"They'll be cheaper at the grocery store," said Paulo. "That's where we should head as soon as we're dropped off."

"Good idea," agreed Gordon.

It was a two hour ride to the city, and unfortunately for us, my dad spent an hour and fifty nine minutes of the ride warning us all about the dangers of the city. We were told to stick together at all times, (even when going to the bathroom), avoid strangers, watch out for pickpockets, thieves and muggers, keep our money hidden and about one hundred other things our parents had been telling us since we were little. Sometimes I really wish parents came with an On/Off button. After all, we aren't babies. We know how to take care of ourselves. Gordon had the $100.00 safely hidden in the back pocket of his jeans, where no pickpocket, thief or mugger could possibly get it. We were way too smart for any city criminals.

We finally arrived in the city and my dad dropped us off in front of the stadium.

"I'll be back in three hours," my dad reminded us. "Meet me right here after the game."

"Thanks for the ride," said Paulo.

"Bye, dad!" I shouted, slamming the door before he could add anything else to his list of warnings about crime in the big city.

"We still have some time before the game starts," said Gordon. "Let's head to the nearest grocery store and get some cold drinks."

We walked about three blocks until we found a grocery store and entered the huge building. It was at least twice the size of anything in our town, and we wandered around for a few minutes before we finally found the beverage aisle.

"Pssst!" whispered Gordon. "Don't look, but I think we're being followed!"

Paulo and I immediately turned around.

"I don't see anyone following us," I said. "You're just paranoid because of my dad's lecture in the car."

"No, I'm sure we're being followed," insisted Gordon. "I'll prove it. Come with me." Gordon ducked into the frozen food aisle. A minute later he stole a glance over his shoulder.

"There she is again! *Don't look!*" he warned.

"Who? That old lady?" I asked, turning around.

"Yes," hissed Gordon. "She followed us into the store, and then she was behind us in the beverage aisle, and now she's coming toward us again!"

"Gordon, that old lady's not a mugger," said Paulo. "We're supposed to watch out for thieves and pickpockets, not old ladies!! What harm can she do?"

"Excuse me," the old lady said in a shaky voice, causing the three of us to practically jump out of our skins.

"I noticed you boys when you first came into the store," she said. Gordon shot us a look that said, *See? I told you!*

"I'm sorry for following you around. It's just that you remind me so much of my poor grandson," she continued, pointing to Gordon.

"Me?" said Gordon.

"Yes. He looks just like you. The same hair colour, the same height, even the same haircut," she sighed. "He moved away last year and I never get to see him anymore." She looked at us with watery eyes.

"That's awful," said Gordon. "You must miss a great kid like that."

"Yes, I do. I was wondering…if it wouldn't be too much trouble, do you think you could say good-bye to me when I'm leaving the store, and maybe call me 'grandma' so I can pretend it's really him?"

"Sure," said Gordon. "If it will make you feel better."

"Oh, I know it will," said the old lady.

We got our drinks and then followed the old lady to the line up at the check-out counter. She went first, slowly putting her groceries on the counter to be rung in. Gordon, Paulo and I picked out some candy while we waited our turn. The old lady scooped up her bags and started to walk away. Then she turned and waved to Gordon.

"Good-bye, dear!" she called out sweetly.

Gordon waved and called out in a loud, clear voice,

"Good-bye, grandma!" and the old lady left the store. Through the front window of the store we could see her get into a taxicab. She slammed the door shut and it quickly sped away.

The cashier rung in our three drinks and chocolate bars and then it happened. "That'll be ninety-eight dollars and sixty-three cents, boys," she said.

"What? For three drinks and three chocolate bars? I think you've made a mistake," protested Gordon.

"No," said the cashier. "Your sweet old grandmother said you'd be paying for her groceries today, too."

Chapter 2

The Substitute

It was a typical Thursday morning at Danglemore Public School. Kids ran around the schoolyard waiting for school to start. At nine o'clock the bell rang and we slowly made our way to the door to line up. When we got there, we noticed that our teacher was absent. That was odd – Mrs. Hoagsbrith rarely missed a day of school. In her place was our principal, Mr. Evans, grinning at us. Now everyone knows that when the principal is smiling, the students are frowning, and if the students are smiling, the principal is the one frowning. From the size of the grin on Mr. Evans' face, it looked like it was going to be a particularly bad day for us.

"Mrs. Hoagsbrith's class, please line up quietly and follow me," announced the principal. We followed him to our classroom and took our seats. Still smiling, he said, "I'll be right back" and he quickly left the room. I detected a definite spring in his step. Yes, this was going to be bad.

Moments later, a beaming Mr. Evans returned with the shiniest substitute teacher I had ever seen. "Class," he said, "Mrs. Hoagsbrith is sick today, but we are honoured to have in her place," he paused for dramatic effect, "Mr. Pompis!" Mr. Evans looked as proud as a new father. "Mr. Pompis has just graduated from the best teacher's college in the country with the highest marks in the school's history. He has a degree in child psychology as well as children's education. It is a privilege to have such a teaching genius in our midst! Please give him a warm welcome."

We stared silently at the teaching genius.

Mr. Evans beamed at us again. As he left the room he added, "No one ever wants to teach your class when your teacher gets sick, but I believe today you've finally met your match."

As the door closed, Mr. Pompis stepped forward and addressed us. "Yes, I understand that this class has been quite a handful over the years, but I'm here to tell you that it's not your fault. As well, I hear that many of you are getting low grades. That's not your fault either."

I could see kids nodding in agreement.

"The reason you've been acting up and getting low marks is because your teachers don't really understand kids."

Our class broke into spontaneous, enthusiastic applause. Finally, someone who knew what he was talking about! I was beginning to like this guy.

"You see," said Mr. Pompis in a confiding tone, "the teachers and principal in this school are simply out of date with modern education. In short, they know very little about teaching students at all. And considering the age of some of these teachers, I'm surprised any of you can even read and write. Today, with my guidance, you are finally going to get to see what teaching and learning are all about!"

Our class leapt to its feet and gave Mr. Pompis a standing ovation. We had all long suspected that our low marks might be our teachers' faults.

When the applause and cheers died out and we had taken our seats, Mr. Pompis continued. "Now the first step in dealing with children is to show them clearly who is the master and who is the student. To prove to you that I am simply the smartest person and best trained teacher you have ever met, I will allow each of you to ask me one question. Anything at all. Something you have always wondered about yet your teachers could never provide an answer. This will prove to you my intellectual superiority."

Our class was clearly impressed. Finally, a teacher that had some answers! Everyone's hand was waving wildly in the air. Mr. Pompis smiled confidently at us and pointed to Gordon. "Yes, what have *you* always wanted to know?"

"Well," said Gordon with a puzzled expression, "I've always wondered why they nail down the lids on coffins."

I thought I noticed the substitute teacher's smile fade just a little. "Hmmm," he said, loosening his tie. "What an interesting question. Well…that's because…

because…um…"

Before Mr. Pompis could wow us with his genius on the subject of coffins, I impatiently blurted out, "Sir, why do they call it a boxing ring when it's really a square?"

Mr. Pompis turned to me, his shiny smile wearing off a little more. "I think, well, ah…"

"What's another word for *synonym*?" blurted out Paulo.

Mr. Pompis undid the top button on his shirt.

"Mr. Pompis," called out a girl from the back of the room. "Why do they call it lipstick, when I can still move my lips after I've used it?"

Mr. Pompis' smile had been completely replaced with a frown. He took a step or two toward the door as the class continued calling out questions.

"Why doesn't glue stick to the inside of the bottle?"

"Why is there a light in the fridge but not the freezer?"

"Why is "abbreviated" such a long word?"

Mr. Pompis took a few more steps toward the door as the barrage continued, and then it happened. He suddenly threw open the door and broke into a run, racing down the hall and out of the school. Mr. Evans just happened to look up as the world's greatest teacher flew by his office.

"Hey!" he shouted. "HEY! WAIT!" The principal jumped out of his chair and gave chase. Our class gathered around the window as Mr. Evans pursued Mr. Pompis across the playground and out to the parking lot, but it was no contest. In a remarkable display of speed, Mr. Pompis easily outdistanced our old principal. He jumped into his car and sped out of the parking lot, the loose gravel flying behind him as he went.

"Well, I don't know about being the world's smartest teacher," said Gordon as the dust settled. "But he sure is the fastest. I've never seen Mr. Evans lose a substitute teacher so quickly before!"

Chapter 3

Three On Three

When something in life seems too good to be true, it usually is. Earlier in the week, Gordon, Paulo and I had been watching TV when a commercial came on announcing a junior boys three on three basketball tournament. The grand prize was *$1000.00!* The catch was that the tournament was being held in a city a couple of hours away, but although our parents gave us permission to go, none of them were free to drive us that day. If we wanted to go, they said, we would have to take the train - and pay for it ourselves. We had our own money, so that was no problem, or so we thought.

The day of the tournament arrived and we headed off to the train station. With any luck, we would return that evening $1000.00 richer. Gordon, Paulo and I were excellent basketball players, and Gordon said he'd bet anyone that the city boys couldn't even spell basketball, much less play it.

We waited in line to buy our train tickets and when it was our turn, Gordon stepped up to the counter and said, "Three return tickets to the city, please."

"That'll be one hundred and eighty five dollars even," said the man.

"One hundred and eighty five dollars!" exclaimed Gordon. "But we've only got $36.00 between us."

"Well, that'll only get you one ticket one way," said the man. "Sorry."

Our dream of winning the basketball tournament was dashed. We sat down sadly on a bench outside the station before returning home.

Suddenly Gordon sat up. "Hey!" he exclaimed. "I've got a great idea!"

Gordon rushed back into the station and came out a few minutes later with one one-way ticket.

"How's that going to help us?" I asked.

"No time to explain," called Gordon over his shoulder. "The train's about to leave. Come on!"

Exchanging puzzled glances, Paulo and I followed Gordon onto the train. We no sooner sat down than the train pulled away from the station. Within a few minutes, a voice announced over the speakers that a conductor would be coming around shortly to take our tickets.

"Follow me," whispered Gordon, heading for the tiny washroom at the back of the compartment. As we squeezed in and closed the door behind us, the "Occupied" light above the door clicked on.

Minutes later, a conductor entered the compartment and began taking people's tickets. Noticing the 'Occupied' sign above the washroom door, he knocked and said, "Ticket, please". Gordon opened the door a crack and slipped our one and only ticket through.

"Thank you," said the conductor and he moved on to the next compartment.

We waited a few minutes longer before opening the door and returning to our seats.

"Well, Gordon, I have to hand it to you," I said with admiration. "You're a genius."

"Yeah," agreed Paulo. "But how are we going to get home tonight? We're broke!"

"Oh, that's easy," said Gordon. "When we win the basketball tournament we'll have more than enough cash to get home."

Paulo and I glanced at each other. "You mean," said Paulo, "that if we don't win the tournament, we'll be trapped in the city with no way home!? Gordon, you're not a genius. You're an idiot!"

Gordon shrugged his shoulders. "Maybe you're right. I didn't have time to plan that far ahead."

Just then, three tall kids sitting across the aisle from us got our attention.

"Hey,' the tallest one said. "That was a pretty clever trick you pulled with the ticket – paying for one and getting three people on. Did we hear you say you were going to the basketball tournament in the city?"

"That's right," said Paulo.

"So are we," said the shortest of the three, who had to be at least a head taller than any of us.

"You can't!" laughed Gordon. "It's a *junior* tournament. You guys are too old to enter."

"Yeah, well, we could use the thousand bucks. We've got our kid brothers' ID and we're going to tell them we're just big for our age."

"But that's cheating, and it's wrong," said Gordon.

"Yup. Sort of like three guys getting on a train with one ticket."

Gordon, Paulo and I rode the rest of the way in silence. We were doomed. There was no way we could beat these guys. They were all well over six feet tall. Man, I hate cheaters!

Our bad luck continued. In the very first round of the tournament we were chosen to play the high school kids from the train. Talk about irony. We were easily beaten and out of the tournament before it barely began. As if losing weren't enough, we now had no way to get home.

The high school kids continued to win game after game until they had won the tournament and our $1000.00 prize. We followed them back to the train station at the end of the day and watched as they purchased one ticket. They were going to try Gordon's trick and save money by buying only one ticket and sneaking on board!

Gordon approached them. "Being as you basically cheated us out of winning that tournament and seeing how you're using *my* trick to get on the train for the price of one, do you think you could buy us one ticket so we could get home, too?"

His question was answered with loud laughter. "Forget it, losers! Find your own way home!!"

Once again, Gordon, Paulo and I found ourselves sitting on a bench outside the train station with no way of getting aboard. And then it happened. Gordon suddenly brightened and said, "I've got a great idea! Come on. Follow me."

"But Gordon—" I began.

"No time to explain. The train's about to leave!"

Paulo and I had no time to argue. With no tickets, we quickly boarded the train behind Gordon and sat down in the compartment behind the one the high school kids had entered.

"Come on," whispered Gordon. "But don't let them see you."

Following Gordon, Paulo and I crept into the next compartment and sat down in the last row of seats. Grabbing some magazines that had been left on the seats, we hid behind them and waited. When the announcement was made that the conductor would be around shortly to collect tickets, the high school kids stood up and headed into the small washroom and closed the door behind them.

"I don't think we were spotted," said Gordon quietly, and a few moments later he got up and walked back to the washroom where the three high-school boys were hiding.

Gordon knocked on the door and said in a deep voice, "Ticket, please."

The door opened a crack and out came the ticket. "Thank you," said Gordon as he took the ticket.

Paulo and I quickly got up and followed Gordon into the next compartment. We headed straight for the washroom and locked ourselves in. Within a few minutes the *real* conductor knocked on the door and said, "Ticket, please." Gordon opened the door just enough to slip the ticket out. "Thank you," said the conductor and continued on his way.

When we were fairly certain he had left our compartment and moved on to the next one, we opened the door and followed him.

"This ought to be good," said Gordon.

We ducked down in the very last seat and watched the conductor going up the aisle collecting tickets. The three high school kids, who thought the conductor had already passed through their compartment, were sitting comfortably in their seats. They were startled to see him approach them and ask for their tickets.

"But we already gave you our ticket, I mean, tickets," stammered one of them.

"I don't think so," said the conductor suspiciously. "I haven't been in this compartment yet."

"Yes, you were. A few minutes ago. We were in the washroom. I mean, I was in the washroom, and I handed you my ticket through the door," said the biggest kid, clearly intending to let his friends fend for themselves.

"Hey, wait a minute!" demanded one of his friends angrily. "Who says that was *your* ticket?"

"I don't see *any* ticket" interrupted the conductor. "So unless you can produce three tickets right now, I'm afraid I'm going to have to ask all of you to get off this train." He waited for a few seconds before the high school kids finally admitted that they had no tickets.

"But I told you," protested the first kid as the conductor helped the boys to their feet and steered them toward the back of the train. "I already gave you my ticket!"

"Shut up, Dylan!" ordered one of his friends. "If we're getting kicked off this train, you're getting kicked off with us."

Gordon, Paulo and I shook with silent laughter as the train came to a stop and then started on its way again a few minutes later, minus the three high school boys.

"Don't you just hate cheaters?" asked Gordon as he waved out the window at the three angry high school kids.

Chapter 4

The Snake

When you hang around with Gordon, you never know when he is going to get a good idea. It can happen anytime, anyplace. His latest great idea happened when he and Paulo and I walked past a streetlight and noticed that someone had put up a sign that said "Lost Dog." Below was the dog's picture, his name and a number you could call if you found the dog.

Paulo said, "There's nothing sadder than a lost dog sign."

"Yep," I agreed. "I sure hope they find him."

Gordon nodded his head in agreement and then paused. "Did you ever notice how it's only cats and dogs that ever get lost, and not some exotic pet?"

"Like what?" I asked.

"I don't know. Something more dangerous that would get everyone in town worried. That would be pretty funny, I'll bet."

"You mean like a snake?" Paulo suggested.

"That's it!" cried Gordon. "A huge poisonous snake. Wouldn't it be fun to put up some lost snake signs around town and see what happens?"

It was a great idea. We went to my house and got to work making lost snake posters. They looked like this:

LOST

One 3 foot long pet rattlesnake.

Answers to the name of Fang

If seen, do not approach as it is very, very poisonous.

Please call: 666-238-1754

The best part was that Gordon smudged the last two numbers in the phone number so that no one could phone the number for more information.

That night, Gordon, Paulo and I had a sleepover in a tent in my backyard. When we were sure my parents were sound asleep, we snuck out with our poisonous snake posters and taped them to streetlights, mail boxes and bulletin boards around town. Our work for the night now done, we pedalled back to my house and crawled into our sleeping bags, hoping that in the morning, at least one person might notice our signs.

Morning came sooner than we expected. It was just after sunrise when Gordon, Paulo and I were awakened to the sound of the tent zipper loudly unzipping. An arm reached into the tent, grabbed me by the scruff of my t-shirt and yanked me out of the tent, still inside my sleeping bag. There stood my mother, one hand clutching me, the other clutching a large frying pan.

"What did I do now? I asked groggily.

"Wake up, boys!" she yelled. "Get out of the tent this minute! Run into the house!!" She let go of me long enough to shake the tent with one hand and to jab at the long grass beside the tent with the frying pan, as though trying to frighten something away.

Gordon and Paulo stumbled out of the tent, still half asleep.

"What's the matter?" asked Paulo, rubbing his bleary eyes. "What time is it?"

"What's going on, mom?" I asked.

"Stop talking and get in the house!" she ordered. "Some fool in this town was keeping a huge poisonous snake for a pet and it escaped!! The whole town is under quarantine. We're all to stay in our houses until the snake has been caught!"

Gordon, Paulo and I shot questioning glances at each other. Should we tell her the truth? Common sense prevailed and we decided to keep quiet.

Mom herded us into the house and flicked on the TV.

"It's been on the news all morning. See if they've found it yet while I go and make you some breakfast. And don't leave the house!"

"Cool!" exclaimed Gordon after she had left the room. "We made it on the news!"

"You'd better hope 'we' *didn't* make the news," said Paulo. "If they find out that this is all just a prank, we're going to be in major trouble. Again," he added, glaring at Gordon.

"Don't blame me," said Gordon. "You're the one that thought up the idea of a lost snake."

"This is no time for arguing," I interrupted. "We need a plan."

"Our plan should be to keep our mouths shut," said Gordon.

And that's what we did.

Gordon and Paulo spent the day indoors at my house while every available city worker searched for the lost poisonous snake. By dusk, they had found nothing and just about everyone in town had cabin fever from being cooped up all day. The mayor and the Chief of Police came up with what they called "Plan B."

Plan B was simply that all available men in town were to report to the soccer field, bringing with them baseball bats, pitchforks, nets, flashlights and whatever else they might need to hunt for the snake.

"Plan B is a wild goose chase," said Paulo. "They won't find anything because there's nothing to find."

"I almost wish there was a real snake and that they'd find it so we could go outside again. I'm getting mighty bored sitting around inside," I said.

A gleam came into Gordon's eye and he leaned closer. "Guys," he said. "I've got a great idea!"

"Not again," moaned Paulo.

"No. This is foolproof. You know that fake rubber rattlesnake I have? Well, it looks just like a real snake, right?"

"Yeah," I said cautiously.

"So, we'll use it as bait and let the men think they've caught the real snake. Then we'll be allowed to go out again."

"Gordon, nobody's going to mistake a rubber snake for a real one," argued Paulo.

"Sure they will. How smart are the mayor and the Chief of Police anyway? Besides, it's dark out. They'll never know the difference."

I wasn't convinced, and I could tell by the look on his face that Paulo wasn't convinced either. Nonetheless, we agreed to go along with Gordon because we couldn't think of a better plan.

Gordon called his mother and asked her if Paulo and I could spend the night at his house. She agreed and twenty minutes later she pulled up in front of my house to pick us up.

"Bye, mom!" I yelled, pulling the front door shut behind us. We ran to the curb and jumped into the van.

When we arrived at Gordon's house, we headed straight for Gordon's room, where we were going to 'play computer games' for a while. Nod, nod. Wink, wink.

Once inside his room, Gordon rummaged around in the closet until he found the rubber snake and his fishing rod.

"What's that for?" I asked.

"We're going to hide in the bushes and cast the snake near the men. Then I'll cut the line and we can run for it."

29

I had to hand it to Gordon. His plan sounded great.

Lowering ourselves out of Gordon's bedroom window with the rope he keeps handy for just that purpose, the three of us snuck through the Smith's backyard and headed toward the soccer field.

When we arrived at the field, we could see a large group of men holding flashlights, torches, pitchforks and nets. They were crowded around the mayor, who was pointing and giving directions.

"OK," whispered Gordon as we crouched behind the bushes at the edge of the field. "No one's looking over here. I'll cast the snake as close as I can to the mayor, cut the line, and we'll run for it. It's dark, so even if they do see us, they won't recognize us."

With a beautiful overhead cast, Gordon dropped the snake about a metre behind the mayor. All the men saw it and yelled at once, "SNAKE! SNAKE!" Several men tripped over each other in their haste to get away from the large poisonous snake. Other braver men charged forward, practically trampling the mayor to get at the snake.

Searching for the snake, someone shone their flashlight into the bushes right near our hiding spot before Gordon could cut the line and we could make our getaway. And then it happened. Someone spotted us!

"Hey, look! Over there!! *I see some kids!*" someone shouted.

"What are you kids doing out? Don't you know there's a snake on the loose!" yelled another man.

"Run for it!!" hissed Paulo, tearing out of the bushes, with me hot on his heels. Gordon followed us, still firmly clutching his fishing rod. The rubber snake bounced along after us.

"LOOK! THE SNAKE'S AFTER THEM!!" cried one of the men, and the chase was on!

In their effort to save us from the big poisonous snake, the men put on a burst of speed that could have set a new Olympic record. Gordon, Paulo and I ran for all we were worth, heading down the dark path toward Lovers Lane.

"Lose the snake!" I panted. "Drop the rod, Gordon!"

"It's my best rod!" protested Gordon.

As though he were running a relay race, Paulo reached out his hand and grabbed the rod from Gordon, flinging it with all his might. The rod landed on the roof of a parked car, and the fake snake dangled into the car through the moon roof! Screaming erupted from inside the car and two teenagers sprinted out as though shot from a cannon screaming, *"SNAKE! SNAKE!"*

Gordon, Paulo and I jumped into the ditch to hide just as the mob of snake hunters burst into the clearing.

"It's in my car!" shouted the teenage boy.

"GET IT!" yelled the mob, attacking the car.

Gordon, Paulo and I decided that now would be a good time to make our getaway. We snuck along the ditch until we reached the main road, and then ran straight to Gordon's house and climbed back into his room through the window. We lay breathless on his floor for a full five minutes before Paulo finally broke the silence.

"Remind me to *never* listen to another one of your ideas again, Gordon!"

"That goes double for me," I added.

"Relax," said Gordon. "We didn't get caught, did we?"

The next morning, as the three of us rode our bikes to the store, we saw another poster attached to the telephone pole. This one wasn't advertising a lost cat or dog. It was a picture of three kids running in the dark, one with something that looked suspiciously like a fishing rod in his hand. You couldn't see the three kids' faces, and the picture was slightly blurry. Above the picture was the large caption: **WANTED!**

"Relax," said Gordon coolly. "It could be anybody."

Chapter 5

The Three 'Bares'

Every year at our school, the older kids put on plays for the little kids in Kindergarten. This year we would be bringing nursery rhymes and fairytales to life. We were put in groups and given our assignments. Some kids were to perform Little Red Riding Hood, while others were to portray the Three Little Pigs. Gordon, Paulo and I hoped we wouldn't be put in any group at all because rehearsals were being held on Saturdays, and since it was April, fishing season was starting. The river would probably be full of fish! Luck was against us, however, and we were put in a group that was to perform Goldilocks and the Three Bears. Gordon, Paulo and I were assigned the role of the three bears. We tried everything we could think of to get out of the play, but it was no use. No matter how badly we performed our parts, Mrs. Hoagsbrith *insisted* that we play the three bears.

We had been practising for two Saturdays in a row, and it was now time for our dress rehearsal. Bright and early on Saturday morning, my mother dropped me off at Paulo's house. Paulo's mother had made us matching bear costumes out of brown fake fur, complete with leather on the paws and plastic claws. They were extremely realistic looking. The costumes were also thick and heavy. If we wore our clothes underneath them, we'd be sweating in no time, so we decided to strip down before getting into them. Then we admired ourselves in the mirror. Although we didn't want to be in a play in the first place, we had to admit that we looked great in our costumes and we couldn't wait for the kids at school to see us.

"Wow!" exclaimed Gordon. "Your mom really did a fantastic job on these costumes. They're so realistic I'll bet we could fool a *real* bear!"

Since the rehearsal didn't start for almost an hour, we decided to ride our bikes to school, taking the long way past the river to see if we could spot any fish. We planned to spend all day Sunday fishing. We left our bear costumes on to save time and jumped on our bikes and headed off.

Once at the river, we left our bikes by some bushes and continued on foot, exploring all of our usual fishing spots along the way. To our delight, there were fish jumping and splashing everywhere. Sunday was going to be a great day! And then it happened. Off in the distance we heard what sounded like a pack of dogs howling.

"Hey, guys," I said. "Do you hear that?"

"Yeah," said Paulo. "It sounds like dogs. A lot of dogs."

"So?" said Gordon, peering into the water at a large fish.

"It sounds like they're running in our direction. The noise is getting louder," I said, just a little scared.

In fact, the pack of dogs was getting closer. We looked back up the riverbank and sure enough, about eight large dogs appeared, sniffing the ground, obviously tracking something. A couple of hunters came into view behind them.

"Hmmm," said Gordon, looking up. "I wonder what they're hunting at this time of year?"

"The only season open right now is...oh, my gosh!!"

"BEAR SEASON!" we all shouted in unison.

"RUN!!" yelled Gordon, and we all ran for it.

Spotting our movement, the dogs began howling again and raced after us. Gordon, Paulo and I ran deeper into the woods, hoping to lose the dogs in the dense trees, but it was no use. They were closing in on us by the second, the hunters following close behind. We were doomed.

Gasping for air, Gordon said, "Quick! We've got to get out of these costumes! The dogs think we're really bears!"

Frantically, we tore off our costumes and threw them on the ground. Then we dove behind some thick bushes, completely naked, just as the pack of howling dogs burst into the clearing.

Our trick worked! The dogs stopped at the bear costumes, growling and barking. They looked puzzled as they sniffed the costumes, and then they began to tear at them!

"Oh, no!" gasped Paulo. "My mom's going to kill us!"

"We've got to get out of here before those dogs do the same to us!" I said.

As quietly as we could, we crept away from the clearing, keeping low so the dogs wouldn't spot us. When we were far enough away, we broke out into a full run, and we didn't stop until we came to the edge of the woods.

"What do we do now?" asked Paulo. "We can't very well go to school *naked!*"

"We can't go *anywhere* like this!" I said. We both turned to Gordon.

"Well, we can't stay here forever," he said. "We'll have to try and make our way back to Paulo's house without being seen."

"How?" I demanded.

"We'll start by staying at the edge of the woods and making our way back in the direction we came from. Then we'll... well, I don't know what we'll do then, but it's a start, anyway. Come on."

Since we had no better ideas, Paulo and I followed Gordon. We walked for about twenty minutes and then we came upon a clearing.

"Look over there!" shouted Paulo. "Do you see what I see?"

Off in the distance was a farmhouse, and flapping in the breeze was a line of freshly washed clothing hanging out to dry!

There didn't seem to be anyone outside at the farmhouse, so we quietly crept toward the yard and climbed carefully over the fence. Ducking behind a swing set, we looked around to make sure the coast was clear, and then we made our way over to the clothesline.

"These are all girls' clothes!" said Paulo in a horrified whisper. "Where are the boys' clothes?"

"Maybe they don't have any boys," said Gordon as he pulled a pink dress off the line and handed it to me. Like a hot potato, I quickly passed it to Paulo. "Here!" I said. "Pink's not my colour."

"I hope you like flowers," said Gordon, yanking down a bright bathrobe covered in red and purple roses. He found a matching nightgown and pulled it over his head while I wrapped the bathrobe around me.

The three of us raced from the yard with a backward glance to make sure we hadn't been spotted and headed toward the road.

We made it to town a few minutes later, trying our best to stay out of sight by ducking behind buildings, parked cars and garbage cans. As we waited for the light to change so we could cross the street, we heard a horn honking. We stared in horror as Mrs. Hoagsbrith waved at us from her car! We had been caught wearing girls' clothes in public by our teacher!! She rolled down her window.

"Well, well, well. What have we here?" she asked, grinning at us. "I thought you three were going to play the three bears? I'll bet the rest of the class would just love to see you dressed up like girls! Get in the car and I'll drive you to school."

"Not dressed like this!" protested Gordon as Mrs. Hoagsbrith opened the back door for us. Then we saw them, our bear costumes, lying on the back seat.

"Our costumes!" shouted Paulo. "How did they get in here?"

"My husband was out hunting this morning and he found them in the woods. They're hardly damaged at all. I figured you boys would try to find some way to get out of doing that play! I'll make you a deal. You boys put these bear costumes back on and be the best three bears anyone has ever seen, and I won't tell a soul how cute you looked running through town dressed as girls!"

Chapter 6

Outhouse With A View

Now that the school play was finally over, Gordon, Paulo and I were looking forward to our first fishing trip of the season. At dawn on Sunday morning, Paulo's dad dropped us off at a heavily wooded spot on a dead end road by a creek. We had never fished this spot before, and we enjoyed a great morning catching fish after fish in the creek. We had wandered quite a way along the creek and as we rounded a bend we were surprised to find a large meadow rising up into a high hill. At the top of the hill there was a tiny building that looked like an outhouse.

"You don't suppose that really is an outhouse way up there?" asked Paulo.

"It sure looks like one to me," I said.

"But why would anyone build an outhouse out in the middle of nowhere?"

"I don't know why," said Gordon. "But I'm glad they did. I really have to go. You guys coming with me?"

"I don't want to climb all that way for nothing," I said.

"We'll wait here and keep fishing," added Paulo.

Gordon leaned his fishing rod against a tree and removed his backpack, setting it down beside his rod. Then he began the five minute walk across the meadow and up the hill to the outhouse. Arriving at the top at last, he looked around and discovered that there was a magnificent view in all directions. Gordon decided to leave the outhouse door open so he could enjoy the terrific view.

Looking up the hill a few minutes later I was surprised to see Gordon sitting in the outhouse, his pants and underwear around his ankles. And then it happened. Before I could say, "Hey, Paulo, get a load of Gordon sitting in the outhouse," I noticed some movement just behind the small building.

"Hey, Paulo, look! A bear!!" I exclaimed, pointing up the hill. Sure enough, a large bear was sniffing around the back of the outhouse!

Paulo and I tried warning Gordon to close the door, but he couldn't hear us shouting from so far away. The bear was now sniffing the side of the outhouse. Seeing Gordon's feet sticking out of the outhouse, he became curious and stuck his big shaggy head into the open door frame, practically on Gordon's lap!

Gordon let loose a yell that I swear must have been heard all the way back in town and slammed the door shut! Like a cork shot from a bottle, the bear did two complete backwards somersaults and then bolted across the meadow and out of sight. When we were sure the bear was gone for good, Paulo and I hiked up the hill and knocked on the outhouse door.

Still shaking, Gordon came out and said, "Did you see that bear?"

"Yeah," said Paulo. "I'll bet you were scared!"

"Well," said Gordon. "Let's just say it was a good thing I was sitting where I was at the time!"

Chapter 7

Gordon To The Rescue

It was Friday afternoon and school had just ended. The fair had come to town and Paulo and I, like many other kids, were on our bikes heading down to the fair grounds. Gordon, however, was serving a detention at school and would be joining us later. Earlier that day, a man had come to our school to talk about the environment and what we could do to help save the planet. After we had gathered in the auditorium, our principal introduced us to a serious looking man who was to be that afternoon's guest speaker. We applauded politely as the tall thin man took centre stage and waited for the applause to die down. Then, without saying a word, he clapped his hands together once. He stood in the middle of the stage and waited. We sat in our seats and waited. After a few seconds passed, the man clapped his hands again, just once. Then he waited again in silence. This was repeated three more times before the guest speaker finally spoke.

"Every time I clap my hands together," he said in a slow, serious tone, "an acre of the rainforest disappears forever."

"*Then quit clapping!!*" shouted a voice from the back of the auditorium. The audience burst out laughing. Every kid in the school knew whose voice it was, but the principal jumped up onto the stage and shouted, **"WHO SAID THAT?"** in his loudest voice.

The audience was suddenly silent. I knew that no one would tell on Gordon. He was too well liked by everyone.

"If I don't have an answer, then the whole school will get *double* the amount of homework for a month!"

Hundreds of fingers automatically pointed to Gordon, who got up from his chair and followed the principal out into the hallway to begin the detention that would keep him from joining Paulo and me at the fair for at least an hour.

It was a hot June day and the fair was at the opposite end of town, at the bottom of what is known as 'Killer Hill.' The reason it was called 'Killer Hill' was because it was a killer to bike down, so just about everyone walked their bike down the hill. Getting back up was even harder. Gordon, Paulo and I have mastered the knack of riding our bikes down the hill by applying just enough pressure on our brakes to slow us down, but not so much pressure that we go flying head over heels. It was a delicate balance that most people wouldn't even attempt.

Arriving safely at the bottom, Paulo and I parked our bikes and checked out the entire fairgrounds. The fair was quite crowded, so we decided not to wait for Gordon before going on a few rides. The lines would only get longer as the day went on.

We were on the top of the Ferris wheel when Paulo suddenly pointed and said, "Look! Is that smoke over there?"

I quickly zeroed in on the direction he was pointing and noticed puffs of black smoke in the distance. "I think you're right!" I said.

When the ride was over we jumped out of our seats and followed the large crowd that was now gathering near the smoke.

"FIRE!" people shouted. **"HELP!"**

Breaking into a run, we followed the crowd to investigate the fire. A large tent that housed a display of wooden outdoor furniture had caught on fire, and people were trying to put it out with buckets of water.

Suddenly someone screamed, *"My baby's in there! Somebody, save my little girl!"*

I craned my neck and sure enough, I could just make out a small toddler crying in the centre of the tent. The fire was spreading towards her! Several adults bravely tried to break through the wall of flames to save the little girl, but the smoke was too thick and the fire was spreading too quickly. We could hear the sound of sirens in the distance and knew that help was on its way. Hopefully, the fire trucks would get here before it was too late!

And then it happened! There was a new wailing sound in the distance and everyone turned to see what it was. *It was Gordon, racing fearlessly down 'Killer Hill' on his bike!!*

"AHHHHHHHHH!!" came Gordon's cry as the crowd scrambled madly out of his way, tripping over each other in their haste to clear a path. Gordon flew through the centre of the fairgrounds straight toward the flaming tent and burst through the wall of flames! Extending his right arm, he scooped up the little girl and held her tightly against him like a football. He continued straight through the tent and the wall of fire on the other side before crashing into a row of porta-potties and coming to a dead stop.

Apart from some bruises and minor scrapes, both Gordon and the little girl were unharmed. The crowd rushed over to Gordon and hoisted him up on their shoulders, carrying him around like a true hero. The mother lovingly hugged and kissed her daughter and the little girl's father pressed a hundred dollar bill into Gordon's hands.

"I can't thank you enough!" he said over and over. "You saved my daughter's life!" He shook Gordon's hand furiously up and down for several minutes.

49

When the commotion was over and the crowd dissolved, Paulo and I picked up Gordon's bike and wheeled it over to him.

"Wow, Gordon," I said. "You really are a hero!"

"I sure was impressed!" said Paulo with true admiration. "What are you going to do with all that money, Gordon?"

"The first thing I'm going to do," said Gordon firmly, "is get the brakes on that darn bike fixed!!"

Chapter 8

The Talent Show Disaster

At the end of every school year, Danglemore Public School holds a talent show in the gym. Kids can sing and dance and some play the piano or the guitar. A few of the older kids in Grade 8 get together and put on funny skits, usually imitating teachers or even the principal. The school band plays something unrecognizable, and some of the teachers even get up on stage and sing. It's a lot of fun, but lacking in any real talent, Gordon, Paulo and I never volunteer to go on stage. We prefer to sit in the audience and watch - that is, until this year. Gordon surprised us by announcing to Paulo and me that he was going to participate in the annual talent show.

51

"No offence, Gordon," I said. "But what talent have you got, except a talent for getting Paulo and me in trouble?"

"You'll have to wait and see," said Gordon mysteriously.

A week before the talent show, Mr. Evans announced that this year's talent show would be held on the last day of school. Furthermore, he he wanted to have an extra-good show because his boss, Mr. Sharpe, would be coming to watch. Mr. Sharpe was the Director of over 100 schools, and he was a very powerful man. All of the students were told to practise very hard to make sure that this year's show was the best ever.

Gordon was determined to use the talent show as an opportunity to get into Mr. Evans' good books.

"The way I see it," said Gordon, "if I put on an awesome talent act, that will make this Director guy happy, and that will make Mr. Evans very happy. Then, the next time I get in trouble, Mr. Evans will remember what a good job I did, and how good I made him look in front of his boss, and he'll take it easy on me."

Paulo and I still had our doubts. I mean, Gordon was a great guy and our best friend, but besides being able to belch the entire alphabet, we'd never seen him display any special talent.

"I have a secret," Gordon said. "Something I haven't even told you guys about yet. For the last two months, I've been studying to be *a hypnotist!*"

"A hypnotist?" asked Paulo in disbelief.

"Cool!" I said with admiration. "How are you doing it?"

"An old friend of my parents used to be a hypnotist, and he taught me the secret of how it's done. He says I'm very good for my age – that I have a real talent for it."

"What's the secret?" I asked eagerly.

"Well," said Gordon. "I'm not supposed to tell anyone, but you guys are my best friends, so I'll give you hint. It's all in the watch!"

"The watch?" I asked, puzzled.

"Yeah, the watch. A good hypnotist always uses a watch that's at least a hundred years old, and it has to be made of real gold."

"Where are you going to get a watch like that?" asked Paulo. "A watch like that would be expensive."

"From my Uncle Ivan. He has an old gold pocket watch on a gold chain that used to belong to his grandfather – my great grandfather. He let me borrow it to practise with and he says I can use it for the school talent show as long as I take really good care of it and don't let anything happen to it."

*　　*　　*　　*　　*

The day of the talent show finally arrived. Mr. Evans had a special chair reserved in the front row for the Director, Mr. Sharpe, where he could get the best view of the show. Paulo and I sat in the middle of the gym with our class while Gordon waited backstage with all the other performers. We hoped Gordon would do well, but he had refused to let us see his act ahead of time, saying that he wanted to surprise us with his amazing new talent.

The show started and we all clapped loudly for the first act, knowing how important this particular show was for our principal. The kids on stage must have been very nervous knowing that Mr. Sharpe was in the audience, and the extra pressure got to them. Singers forgot the words to their songs, dancers tripped and fell, and our juggler could only juggle two apples. So far, it had to be the worst talent show ever. Mr. Sharpe yawned and looked bored, while Mr. Evans sat beside him, nervous and sweating. Gordon was scheduled to be the last act, and it looked like it was up to him to save the day!

"Our school's last act will be Gordon Smith," sighed Mr. Evans wearily into the microphone as he wiped the sweat off his bald head with a handkerchief. There was thunderous applause in the gym. Gordon was very popular at Danglemore Public School.

Wearing a black magician's cape, Gordon calmly strolled onto the stage, stood up on a chair and raised his arms for silence. "And now," said Gordon in a loud voice, "for my part in the talent show, I will amaze you by hypnotizing an entire group of students. Which class would like to volunteer?"

Instantly every hand in the gym shot up into the air.

"How about this class," said Gordon, pointing to the Grade 2 class in the second row. With the help of their teacher, the little kids were herded up on stage and arranged in a long row in front of Gordon, their backs to the audience. Gordon carefully pulled the expensive gold watch from his pocket. Holding it by the chain, he dangled it in the air and then slowly swung it back and forth in front of the students. All of the kids concentrated as the expensive gold watch swung back and forth, back and forth, in front of them.

"You are getting sleepy," Gordon said in a deep voice. "Your eyes feel heavy and you want to go to sleep." Gordon kept talking slowly and calmly for about a minute, and then we could see a head droop, and then another and another as the entire class actually became hypnotized! I had to admit, I was impressed. The audience was silent as everyone held their breath and watched in amazement.

"Now," said Gordon in the same steady voice while he continued to swing the watch, "everyone, look at the watch." Immediately every head in the Grade 2 class snapped to attention and focused on the expensive gold watch. Gordon began to swing the watch faster.

"On the count of three, I will give you a command. I want everyone to obey my command. One…two…three! Jog on the spot!" ordered Gordon. Immediately, every kid in the class leapt to their feet and began running on the spot!

The audience broke out into spontaneous applause.

"Stop!" commanded Gordon, and the class stopped.

"Flap your arms like a chicken," ordered Gordon. Obediently, the class turned into 20 chickens on stage!

I stole a glace at the Director. He was clapping and smiling. Mr. Evans was smiling, too, for the first time all day. Gordon had saved the show and was well on his way to becoming the principal's favourite student! And then it happened. One of the little kids who was flapping his arms wildly and making clucking sounds got a bit too close to Gordon, and he accidentally knocked the expensive gold watch from his hand, sending it flying across the stage and landing with a crash on the floor! The watch shattered into a thousand tiny pieces!!

"Oh, poop!" exclaimed Gordon loudly.

* * * * *

It took the school custodians 4 hours to clean up the mess on stage. The Director never returned to Danglemore Public School again, and it was the last talent show we ever had.

Chapter 9

Gordon's Lesson

One day near the end of June, Gordon began looking for a summer job to earn some spending money. For days, he pored over the Help Wanted section of the newspaper to find just the right job – something that paid well and wasn't too difficult. Finally he found it; the perfect job.

"Look at this," said Gordon, reading aloud to Paulo and me from the newspaper. *"Wanted: Person to do odd jobs at large home. No experience necessary. Must be hard-working. Apply in person."*

"Well, that lets you out," joked Paulo. "You've never put in a hard day's work in your life."

"Ha! We'll see about that," said Gordon.

That afternoon, Gordon rode his bike to the address listed in the paper. He knocked on the door of a very large mansion in the rich section of town and it was answered by a man wearing a black suit and white gloves.

"I'm here to apply for the job in the newspaper. Are you the man who placed the ad?" asked Gordon.

"I am the butler," replied the man with an English accent. "Come this way." Bowing slightly, he led Gordon into the house and showed him to a chair. Gordon sat down and waited. Glancing around, Gordon could see that everything in the house was very expensive. The person who placed the ad in the newspaper must be extremely rich.

A minute later, a man entered and shook Gordon's hand, introducing himself as Mr. Davis.

"I'm looking for someone to help me out around the place this summer," he explained. "My regular gardener broke his leg, and I need someone to cut the lawn, trim the bushes, vacuum the pool, that sort of thing. The job pays well, and all I ask is that you show up on time and put in an honest day's work. Are you interested?"

"Yes, sir. I am," said Gordon eagerly. "When do I start?"

"How about tomorrow morning, at 8 a.m. sharp?"

"I'll be here," said Gordon. Mr. Davis shook his hand to seal the deal and Gordon was shown out of the house by the butler, who held the door open for him.

The next day, Gordon arrived promptly at 8 a.m. to begin his first day of work.

"Ah, good," said Mr. Davis. "You're on time. I admire that in a person. Today, I'd like you to cut the lawn. It's a big property, so it will take you all day, but you'll be well rewarded on payday at the end of the week."

Gordon immediately got to work pushing the lawnmower up and down the huge front lawn. It was hot, sweaty work, and it took Gordon most of the morning just to get the front lawn done. As he rounded the side of the house and pushed the mower around to the backyard, he could see the rich Mr. Davis lounging beside his glistening swimming pool, sipping a cold drink from a large pitcher of ice water.

Wiping his brow with the back of his arm, Gordon turned off the mower and called out, "Excuse me, Mr. Davis, but do you think I could have a glass of water?"

Mr. Davis took off his sunglasses and studied Gordon for a moment before answering.

"Gordon," he said. "You should have thought to bring your own water bottle with you today. You knew I expected a hard day's work out of you and you should have come prepared. Now, I could give you a nice cold glass of water, but if I did that, you wouldn't learn anything. Tomorrow, bring your own water."

Gordon opened his mouth to reply, but then he thought about that nice big paycheck he was going to get on Friday and decided not to argue. He started the mower again and began cutting the back lawn.

At the end of the day, Mr. Davis seemed very pleased with Gordon's work. He thanked him and told him that tomorrow he wanted Gordon to do some gardening for him. The bushes and hedges all needed trimming. Tired and very thirsty from his long day of cutting grass, Gordon climbed on his bike and headed home.

The next morning, Gordon again showed up promptly at 8 o'clock to begin another long day's work. This time he remembered to bring his own water bottle. Mr. Davis told him how to trim the bushes and left Gordon to get on with his work.

Things went smoothly at first, but then Gordon came to a rose garden. The branches were all covered in thorns, and Gordon's hands quickly became scratched and bloody. Gordon went up to the house and knocked on the back door. It was opened by Mr. Davis himself.

"Sorry to bother you," said Gordon politely. "I'm trimming the roses like you showed me, but my hands are getting cut by all the thorns. Do you think I could borrow a pair of gardening gloves?"

Sighing, Mr. Davis patiently explained that he had told Gordon yesterday that he would be trimming bushes, and that Gordon should have thought ahead and brought his own gardening gloves.

"Of course, I can loan you a pair of my gardener's gloves, but if I do that, then what will you have learned?

Nothing. It's important to always think ahead and be prepared. Now, tomorrow, come prepared."

Muttering to himself, Gordon returned to the rose garden and continued to trim the bushes, being as careful as possible to avoid the thorns. By the end of the day, Gordon's hands were in rough shape, scratched and cut from all his hard work.

"Very nice job," said Mr. Davis, checking Gordon's work. "You're working out just fine. Now tomorrow, I'd like you to weed the gardens for me."

"Alright," said Gordon, thinking that he wouldn't forget his water bottle *or* gardening gloves the next day.

When Gordon arrived for work on the third day, he noticed a large catering van parked outside the mansion. Mr. Davis explained to him that he was hosting a big party that day in the backyard, but that Gordon was to go about his work as usual and try to stay out of the guests' way.

Gordon began weeding the gardens while the caterers got busy setting up tables and chairs for what looked like about a hundred guests. By noon the air was filled with the delicious aroma of food and most of the guests had arrived.

"Those smells sure are making me hungry," thought Gordon. *"I think I'll take my lunch break now."*

Gordon headed towards his bike to get his lunch. Opening up the back carrier, he stared in disbelief. He had forgotten his lunch at home! Sighing, he headed back to work, passing the long tables of food on his way. His mouth watered at the sight of steak and lobster, dinner rolls, salad, and an enormous dessert table piled high with cakes, pies and puddings.

Several hours later, just as Gordon finished his weeding, the last of Mr. Davis' guests drove away and the caterers began clearing the dishes and removing the leftover food.

"What do you do with all the leftovers?" Gordon asked one of the caterers.

"Nothing. We throw them out," he replied.

"Throw them out?" said Gordon. "Then Mr. Davis probably won't mind if I help myself. I forgot my lunch today and I'm starving."

Just as Gordon was reaching out to grab a bun, he heard someone clearing his throat loudly behind him and turned around to find Mr. Davis.

"Gordon," he said in his slow, patient manner. "What are you doing?"

"I didn't think you'd mind. The caterer said this was just going to be thrown out, and I forgot my lunch today and..."

"I see," interrupted Mr. Davis. "And you thought you'd help yourself. I could let you do that, but then what would you have learned? Nothing. Now put down the food."

Gordon put the bun back and stood with his stomach growling while Mr. Davis explained that Gordon would be planting trees the next day.

Early the next morning, Gordon set out with his water bottle, his gardening gloves, and his lunch. He even double checked his bike carrier to make sure he hadn't forgotten anything. It was a cloudy day, but Gordon didn't mind. At least he wouldn't bake in the hot sun.

Mr. Davis told Gordon the correct way to plant the small trees and then left Gordon to get on with his task. By noon, Gordon had planted about a hundred little trees and was ready for a break. As he sat down on the grass and opened his lunch bag, a few drops of rain began to fall, and before long, it was coming down in a steady stream. Gordon ran up to the house and knocked on the door. This time it was opened by the butler.

"Ah," he said in his smooth voice. "Mr. Davis said you might be asking for a raincoat."

"Great!" said Gordon with relief, thinking that for once the rich man was going to help him out.

"He said to tell you that if he gives you a raincoat, you will learn nothing. You should have checked the weather report this morning and then you would have come prepared." The butler closed the door, leaving Gordon standing in the pouring rain.

By the end of the day, Gordon had finished planting all the trees and was soaked to the skin. His teeth chattered as he pedaled his bike home.

"If this job weren't paying so much, I'd quit," he grumbled to himself. "With all the money that guy's got, you think he could have lent me a raincoat! I'll probably catch a major cold after spending the afternoon in the pouring rain."

The next day, Gordon headed off for work in a better mood. The sun was shining and it was payday!

That day, Gordon's job was to vacuum the pool, scrub all the lawn furniture and pick up all the dog droppings from the lawn. Mr. Davis had three large dogs. It was a scorching hot day, but Gordon set to work eagerly. By 11 o'clock, the sun was beating down on him and he could feel the back of his neck begin to burn. He glanced over at Mr. Davis sitting beside the pool with his wife, both covered in sunscreen and sipping cool drinks.

Trying one last time, Gordon said, "Excuse me, Mr. Davis, but it's awfully hot today. Do you think I could use some of your sunscreen? I'm starting to get a burn."

"Of course I could let you use our sunscreen, Gordon," began Mr. Davis. "But you obviously didn't learn anything at all yesterday, did you? Yesterday it poured rain and you got soaked because you didn't check the weather. Today it's hot and sunny and again, you didn't check the weather this morning, did you? No, if I loan you our sunscreen, then you'll never learn anything." He got up and went into the house. His wife looked at Gordon with sympathy.

"Is he always like this?" Gordon asked her.

"I'm afraid so," said his wife. "You see, when he was young, he was very poor and he had to work very hard for everything he has. He did all kinds of jobs, anything to earn a little money. Now he's one of the richest men in town, all because of the lessons he learned when he was young like you. He's really just trying to help you, but it does make me angry, watching you work so hard out here just so that he doesn't have to get his hands dirty. Just once, I'd like to see him do something around this place, instead of ordering other people about."

"That would be funny," said Gordon. "Seeing Mr. Davis getting his hands dirty!"

"I can guarantee you that would *never* happen," said his wife.

"You never know," said Gordon slyly.

*   *   *   *   *

At the end of a long day, Mr. Davis came outside to inspect Gordon's work.

"Well, you've done a great job, Gordon. I'm impressed. And I hope you learned something this week."

"Yes, sir. I sure did," said Gordon.

"Well, here is your paycheck. $200.00. I hope you're planning to do something wise with this money."

"Yes, sir. I'm going to bet it," replied Gordon.

Mr. Davis slammed down Gordon's paycheck on the table. "Bet it! You obviously haven't learned a thing this week! Don't you know that betting is for fools? You'll never get ahead in life by betting! You'll lose everything!"

"Well, I've made some money in the past by betting," said Gordon.

"Give me one example of how you made money by betting," said the man.

"Well," said Gordon. "I'll bet you my entire $200.00 paycheck that you won't pick up that fresh dog dropping over there *with your bare hands.*"

"Let me get this straight," said Mr. Davis. "You want to bet me your entire paycheck that I won't pick up a dog dropping with my bare hands? That's a foolish bet. If I pick up that dog dropping, I get to keep your paycheck and you will have done all this work for nothing!"

"That's right," said Gordon, holding out his hand to shake on the bet. "What do you say?"

"I say you're going to learn a very difficult lesson today," he said, shaking Gordon's hand before walking over and picking up the dog dropping with his bare hands. He held it out to Gordon to make sure there was no doubt that he had won the bet and Gordon had just lost his entire paycheck.

"I hope you've learned a very valuable lesson today, Gordon," said Mr. Davis.

"I sure did!" said Gordon, grinning, and then it happened.

Just then, Mrs. Davis came outside. "I can't believe what I'm seeing!" she cried. "*What* is in your hand?"

"I just taught this young man a very valuable lesson," said Mr. Davis triumphantly. "He bet me his entire paycheck that I wouldn't pick up this dog dropping with my bare hands. Just to prove to him how silly betting is, I did pick it up, and Gordon is $200.00 poorer!"

"No, he's not," said his wife, reaching into her purse for her check book. "You see, earlier today, I told Gordon that

71

you hated to get your hands dirty, and he bet me $500.00 that by the end of today, he could make you pick up a dog dropping with your bare hands!"

"I think that kid outsmarted both of us! He's going to go far in life," said Mr. Davis as Gordon pedaled home with a $500.00 check in his pocket.

Chapter 10

Easy Come, Easy Go

One summer evening, just as it was getting dark, Gordon was biking home from my house. I don't know how he missed it, but somehow he didn't see the silver-blue convertible parked on the side of the road, and he smashed into the back of it at top speed! He was launched head over heels like a human cannonball and landed in the front seat, completely unharmed but dazed. Just as he was opening the door to get out, he heard a man's voice yelling, "Are you alright!?"

"I'm fine," said Gordon with a smile. "Not a scratch on me!"

"Well, that's more than I can say for my car!" said the man. "Look! Your bike made a huge scratch on my '57 Corvette!"

"Gee, I'm sorry," said Gordon, and then he recognized the man. It was the Chief of Police!

"Say, aren't you Gordon Smith?" demanded the Chief, peering at Gordon. "I should have known it was you!"

"It was an accident, really!" said Gordon earnestly.

"I've got a good mind to write you a ticket for careless operation of a bike! Why were you going so fast? What if my car had been a woman pushing a baby carriage? Someone could have been seriously hurt. You're required to have a light on that thing so you can see where you're going! You'll have to pay to get that scratch fixed."

"But I don't have that much money," gulped Gordon.

"Then let's just see what your parents have to say about this," he said, reaching into his pocket and taking out a cell phone. Knowing that there was no way out of the trouble he was in, Gordon gave the man his phone number and ten minutes later, his parents arrived to discuss the situation with the Chief. While his parents, the Chief and his wife sat comfortably in the Chief's backyard sipping iced tea, Gordon sweated it out in the front yard while they decided his fate. An hour and several drinks later, it was decided that the Chief would repair the scratch himself but Gordon would have to make it up to the Chief by doing odd jobs like cutting the grass and washing windows at his house on Saturday.

When Saturday arrived, Gordon biked over to the Chief's house at the crack of dawn to begin a long day of hard labour.

"Now, all the windows in the front *and* the back of the house need washing. Then the lawn needs to be cut, and when you're done that, I want you to clean the pool."

"Oh, man! That will take all day," groaned Gordon.

"Exactly! That's the idea," said the Chief. "My wife and I are going out for the day, and we'll be back at 4:00. After we've inspected your work, you can go home – *if* you've done a satisfactory job. Now let me show you the proper way to clean the pool."

As the Chief demonstrated how the pool was to be cleaned, he said, "Now, there is one other thing I insist on:

No one, and I mean NO ONE, is allowed in the pool. Not you, not your friends, and especially not that no-good brother of mine! Do you understand? If I find out that you let *anyone* go for a swim in this pool, you'll be working every Saturday for the rest of the summer! Is that understood?"

"Perfectly," gulped Gordon. "*No one* is allowed in the pool."

As the Chief and his wife pulled out of the driveway, Gordon got the ladder from the garage, a bucket of water and some rags to begin cleaning the windows. It was hot work, and the sun beat down on Gordon, making him sweat. As he dragged the ladder around the house to begin cleaning the back windows, the water in the pool glistened invitingly.

Boy, thought Gordon. *A quick dip in the pool sure would feel good about now.* Then he remembered the Chief's words. *No one* is allowed in the pool. Sighing, Gordon climbed the ladder and began washing the next window.

Two hours later, hotter and stickier than before, Gordon put the ladder away and took a short break for lunch.

Maybe I could just dangle my feet over the side, he thought, but the words of the Police Chief came back to him. *No one* is allowed in the pool. *I don't want to spend all summer working here if someone sees me in the pool and tells the Chief.*

Just as Gordon was finishing his lunch, Paulo and I decided to drop in on him to see how the work was progressing.

"Hey, Gordon," I said. "Man, you look hot!"

"Let's have a quick swim and cool off," suggested Paulo.

"Don't you dare!" said Gordon. "If I let anyone near that pool, the Chief is going to make me work for him all summer!"

"Oh, come on. He'll never know," I coaxed.

"No way!" insisted Gordon. "Anyway, I don't have time for a swim. I've got to cut the lawn."

Paulo and I left Gordon to his task and headed down to the river for a swim as he started up the mower and began cutting the lawn in the hot sun.

Just as he was finishing trimming the edges, a car pulled into the driveway. A man got out and Gordon was startled to see him open the gate and come into the backyard.

"Hello!" called out the man. "Allow me to introduce myself. I'm Walter, the Police Chief's brother."

Gordon recognized the man. It was very well known that the Chief and his brother did not like each other. In fact, Gordon had heard that the Chief had even given his own brother a hundred dollar speeding ticket several days ago.

"I'm Gordon. The Chief won't be home until 4:00."

"Yes, I know," said Walter. "I just bumped into him in town. He told me you were working here today because you scratched that precious car of his. I want to ask you a favour. Will you let me have a quick swim in his pool?"

"NO!" shouted Gordon. "I can't. The Chief said that *no one* is allowed in his pool."

"I know," said Walter with a sly grin, "but I'm desperate. I've always wanted to swim in his lovely pool, especially after he gave me that speeding ticket. Heck, I'll even give you $100.00 if you let me have a quick dip."

"Wow! A hundred dollars!" cried Gordon in amazement. "The Chief said that if I let anyone swim in his pool, he'd make me work every Saturday for the rest of the summer, but for a hundred dollars, I can keep a secret! Go ahead, but you've got to be really quick about it!"

"Great! Thanks," said Walter, removing his t-shirt and jumping into the pool in his shorts. He swam several laps and then got out and did a few cannon balls off the diving board.

"Hurry up," warned Gordon. "It's almost 4:00."

"OK, OK. Don't get your shorts in a knot," said Walter, climbing out of the pool and reaching into his wallet to give Gordon his hundred dollars. Then he quickly dried himself off, jumped into his car and sped away.

Before Gordon could put away his money, the Chief came racing up the driveway and screeched to a halt. He leapt out of the car and ran up to Gordon.

"Was that my brother's car I just saw leaving here?" he demanded.

"Well, um... yes. As a matter of fact it was," stammered Gordon.

"Good. I just saw him in town an hour ago and he promised he would drop off the hundred dollars he owes for the speeding ticket I gave him last week. That must be it," he said, spying the money in Gordon's hands. The Chief quickly reached out and snatched up the bills, leaving Gordon open-mouthed and speechless – and one hundred dollars poorer.

Chapter 11

Hamburger Helper

By the middle of July, Gordon had had enough of trying to make money by babysitting babies, dogs and cats. They were too much trouble, he said. Cats ran away, dogs bit, and babies needed their diapers changed. He had discovered an easier way to make money by cutting grass. It was the perfect job. In fact, for the last two weeks, Gordon had been cutting the lawn of an old couple who were no longer able to push a mower and were happy to pay Gordon to do the job for them. They paid Gordon $40.00 to do it each week and it took him four hours. Compared to changing diapers and walking dogs, it was an easy job.

Because Gordon had this great-paying job, he was feeling generous and offered to treat Paulo and me to ice cream at the best ice cream parlour in town before heading off to his grass cutting job one day.

"This is the best job ever," exclaimed Gordon as we stood in line at the ice cream counter. "It pays well and it only takes four hours a week. Cutting grass sure is easier than babysitting or walking people's dogs."

The man in line ahead of us turned around and studied Gordon. "Pardon me," he said. "But did I hear you say you cut lawns?"

Thinking the man must want to hire him to cut his grass, Gordon replied, "Yes, sir. I sure do. Are you interested?"

"Maybe," said the man. "I'd have to see your work first, though. Where did you say you were working?"

"I'm cutting the lawn at 14 Mill Cove," said Gordon. "I'm sure they'll give me a good reference."

"Thanks," said the man, and he hurried out of the ice cream parlour without even buying any ice cream.

"It looks like you've got another customer lined up," remarked Paulo with envy. "I wish I could make $10.00 an hour cutting grass."

Gordon bought us all some ice cream and we sat down to enjoy it before walking Gordon over to Mill Cove to begin his great job.

When we arrived at the elderly couple's house, we were surprised to see a truck with a trailer attached to it parked in front of the house. There was a sign on the truck that said "Econo-Cut. We Cut The Competition!" We could hear the sound of a lawnmower in the distance.

"Hey!" said Gordon. "The front lawn has already been cut, and it sounds like someone is cutting the back lawn, too. This is my job! What's a professional lawn service doing here?"

"I don't know, Gordon, but it looks like they've hired someone else to do the job," I said.

Then, from around the corner of the house, came a big riding lawn mower driven by a man.

"That's the guy from the ice cream store!" I exclaimed.

"He stole my job!" yelled Gordon.

Seeing us, the man turned off the mower, tipped his hat back and said, "Howdy, boys. Nice day for some yard work, eh?"

"You stole my job!" accused Gordon.

"Well, now, I wouldn't put it that way," said the man, slick as oil.

"How would you put it then?" demanded Gordon.

"Well, now. I'd say I outbid you. You see, it takes you four hours to cut this lawn with a push mower, and I can do it in less than half the time, and for less than half the price."

"We'll see about that," said Gordon, heading up the front walk and ringing the doorbell.

"Here comes trouble!" squawked a large white parrot sitting in a cage on the front porch.

"Hi, Captain Riddle," said Gordon to the bird, reaching into his pocket and bringing out the crackers he had brought for him. Captain Riddle was the elderly couple's pet, and they doted on him, feeding him special treats and calling him their "grand-parrot" since they had no grandchildren to spoil.

The door was opened by Mr. Adams, the elderly man who had hired Gordon to cut his lawn. He looked a little uncomfortable to see Gordon standing there.

"Oh, hello, young man," he said, obviously embarrassed. "You're early today."

"I wanted to get a head start on your lawn, but I see *he* beat me to it," said Gordon, gesturing to the man on the riding mower.

"Well, it's like this," said the old man slowly. "This fellow says he can cut our lawn for half of what we were paying you, and well, money's a bit tight, so we thought we'd give him a try. You understand, I'm sure."

"I guess so," mumbled Gordon. "Does this mean I'm fired?"

"I wouldn't put it like that," said Mr. Adams. "Let's just say your services are no longer required."

Gordon turned away and came slowly down the driveway to where Paulo and I waited for him on the curb.

"What did he say?" I asked.

"He said this guy can do it for half the price, and money's tight, so what else could he do? I don't blame him. I blame the guy on the lawn mower! He stole my job!!"

"What a creep!" said Paulo. "You're not going to let him get away with it, are you?"

"What can I..." but before he had even finished his own question, Gordon already had a plan. *"Guys, I've got a great idea!* Will you help me pay back this job thief?"

Eager to see justice done, (and hopefully to get more free ice cream), Paulo and I agreed to help.

*   *   *   *   *

Gordon's plan was simple, but it was pure genius. Gordon had always cut the Adams' lawn on Tuesdays, so he figured that the man from "Econo-Cut" would be back next Tuesday to cut their lawn again. We had to wait a whole week to put Gordon's plan into action, but it was worth the wait.

The following Monday, Gordon went to the grocery store and bought a pound of hamburger meat, which he hid in the back of the fridge so his mother wouldn't find it and cook it for dinner. Next, he undid the seam on his pillow and placed several handfuls of feathers into a bag. Then, he found an old birdcage that was stored in his garage. He was all set.

The next day, Gordon met us around the corner from the Adams' house. We waited for about a half hour and finally, just before lunch time, we saw the truck with the "Econo-Cut" sign pull up to the house. Within a few moments we could hear the drone of the riding lawn mower as the man quickly rode it up and down the front lawn cutting wide strips of grass with each pass. Eventually, he shut the mower off, wiped the back of his hand across his sweaty brow, and walked over to his truck for a cold drink and a short lunch break. Settling back in the driver's seat, he leaned back and closed his eyes to rest and cool off before finishing the job.

"OK," said Gordon. "Now's our chance."

Ducking low, Paulo and I dashed across the lawn to the front porch and gently lifted Captain Riddle out of his birdcage and placed him in the one Gordon had brought from home. We made sure we left the door to Captain Riddle's cage open. Fortunately, we made it back to the hedge around the corner just as the parrot began to talk. *"Here comes trouble! Wraaaak!"*

Meanwhile, Gordon darted up to the riding mower and using a small plastic shovel, he carefully pushed the ground beef and several handfuls of feathers underneath the mower, being careful to keep his fingers well away from the sharp blade. Then he rejoined us behind the hedge to watch the excitement.

"This should be good!" he chuckled, rubbing his hands together in anticipation.

A few minutes later, his break over, the man climbed out of his truck to finish cutting the grass. He sat down on the mower and turned the key. The engine sputtered and came to life, and then it happened. There was a loud thud followed by several more thuds and bangs and then something messy shot out from underneath the mower, followed by a cloud of white feathers!

Startled, the man turned off the engine and climbed down to examine the debris that had flown out from his mower. He bent down and stared and then slowly turned his head and looked toward the front porch of the house to where Captain Riddle's birdcage hung – empty! His head swivelled back to the mess of ground beef and feathers, and then back to the birdcage again. His eyes popped open wide as the realization of what must have happened crept over him. He removed his cap and wiped his brow several times, and then slowly made his way to the front porch to stare into the birdcage, no doubt hoping to find the beloved parrot hiding in a corner of the cage or behind his water dish. Finding the door open and no trace of the parrot in the cage, he reluctantly rang the doorbell and waited for one of the elderly Adams to open it. A moment later Mrs. Adams answered the bell.

"Yes? Are you finished already?" she asked.

"No, not quite, ma'am," began the man. "You see…uh…well, I'm afraid there's been a little accident."

"Oh, I hope you're not hurt!" cried the old woman.

"No, ma'am. It's not me. It's your bird—"

Before he could finish the sentence, the old woman scurried out of the house in her slippers and went straight to the cage.

"Captain Riddle!" she exclaimed. ***"What's happened to my poor parrot?"***

"Well, ma'am, it's like this."

Gordon, Paulo and I watched as the man proceeded to explain about poor Captain Riddle. He gestured to the cage, and then to his lawn mower, and then to the pile of feathers and ground beef! The poor old woman's eyes widened as the tale went on, and her face grew whiter by the second.

"My Poor Captain Riddle!" she cried. **"YOU'VE KILLED CAPTAIN RIDDLE!!"**

"It was an accident, ma'am. I had no idea the bird was underneath the blades when I started the mower up!"

I thought the old woman was going to faint, but instead she starting shouting, **"YOU'RE FIRED! TAKE THAT DARN LAWN MOWER AND GET OFF MY PROPERTY THIS INSTANT!!"**

The man backed away from the front porch, apologizing with each step he took. Gordon, Paulo and I sat hidden behind the hedge, holding our sides as we shook with laughter and silently high-fived each other.

90

"Now," said Gordon when the man from "Econo-Cut" had driven away. "All we have to do is wait a few minutes and then knock on the old lady's door and tell her that we found her parrot flying around the neighbourhood. She'll be so happy to see Captain Riddle that she'll probably give me my job back. Who knows? Maybe I'll even get a raise!"